HASBRO and its logo, MY LITTLE PONY and all related characters are trademarks of Hasbro and are used with permission. © 2015 Hasbro. All Rights Reserved.
Cover design by Kayleigh McCann

In accordance with the U.S. Copyright Act of 1976, the scanning, uploading, and electronic sharing of any part of this book without the permission of the publisher is unlawful piracy and theft of the author's intellectual property. If you would like to use materials from the book (other than for review purposes), prior written permission must be obtained by contacting the publisher at permissions@hbgusa.com. Thank you for your support of the author's rights.

Little, Brown and Company

Hachette Book Group
1290 Avenue of the Americas, New York, NY 10104
Visit us at lb-kids.com
mylittlepony.com

LB kids is an imprint of Little, Brown and Company.
The LB kids name and logo are trademarks of Hachette Book Group, Inc.

The publisher is not responsible for websites (or their content) that are not owned by the publisher.

First Edition: July 2015

Library of Congress Cataloging-in-Publication Data

Alexander, Louise (Louise Shirreffs), 1979–
School spirit! / adapted by Louise Alexander. — First edition.
pages cm. — (My little pony)
"Based on the episode 'Ponyville Confidential' by M. A. Larson."
Summary: "The Cutie Mark Crusaders still don't have their cutie marks! What are their special talents? Could it be writing? The Crusaders join the school newspaper to find out. What will Apple Bloom, Scootaloo, and Sweetie Belle learn at The Foal Free Press?"—
Provided by publisher.
ISBN 978-0-316-41078-6 (pbk) — ISBN 978-0-316-34193-6 (ebook)
I. Larson, M. A. II. Title.
PZ7.A37746Sc 2015   [E]—dc23   2014044011

10 9 8 7 6 5 4 3 2 1

CW

Printed in the United States of America

Licensed By:

School Spirit!

Adapted by **Louise Alexander**
Based on the episode "Ponyville Confidential" by **M. A. Larson**

LITTLE, BROWN & COMPANY
LB kids

The first day of school is over, and Sweetie Belle and Scootaloo are sad.

"I can't believe Featherweight got his cutie mark over summer vacation," Scootaloo says.

"We need to earn our cutie marks!" exclaims Sweetie Belle.

"But *how*?" Scootaloo asks.

Apple Bloom joins them. "Ponies, if we want to be cool, we need to learn from the most popular pony in school, Diamond Tiara," she says.

Since she is the pony in chief of the *Foal Free Press*, the Cutie Mark Crusaders decide to join the school newspaper.

At their first meeting, Sweetie Belle, Scootaloo, and Apple Bloom nervously listen as Diamond Tiara talks about her goals for the newspaper this year.

"I am going to deliver this paper to newfound glory! I want juicy stories—the juicier the better!"

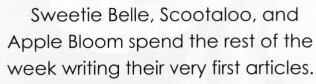

Sweetie Belle, Scootaloo, and Apple Bloom spend the rest of the week writing their very first articles.

Apple Bloom loves history, so she talks to Granny Smith about the early years of Ponyville.

Scootaloo loves nature, so she writes a story about newborn animals.

Sweetie Belle loves fashion, so she interviews Rarity about her newest hat design.

The Cutie Mark Crusaders hand in their stories to Diamond Tiara, but the pony in chief throws the papers back in their faces.

"You call this news?!" she screeches. "Get something else on my desk by the end of the day! And it better be juicy!"

"How are we ever going to find other stories to write by the end of the day?" Scootaloo asks.

Suddenly, Sweetie Belle notices something funny and grabs Featherweight to take pictures.

They catch Snips and Snails sticking to a giant blob of bubble gum! Sweetie Belle knows the photo will make the whole school laugh—and she's right.

The lead story in the next *Foal Free Press* reads:

SNIPS AND SNAILS AND BUBBLEGUM TAILS

The story is by Gabby Gums, the name the Cutie Mark Crusaders use.

The next day, everypony in school is talking about the article! Snips and Snails pretend to be okay, but they are embarrassed.

Diamond Tiara, on the other hand, is thrilled! She congratulates the Crusaders.

"I want more! You are my new top gossip columnists!"

"We really have a gift for gossip, ponies!"
Scootaloo cheers as she high-hooves Sweetie
Belle and Apple Bloom.

Sweetie Belle replies, "If we write a few more
Gabby Gums articles, I know we'll earn our cutie
marks for sure!"

The trio sneaks around Ponyville, looking for more gossip. Other articles appear in the *Foal Free Press* with crazy headlines:

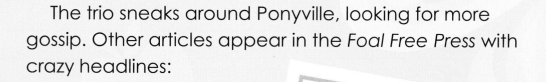

TROUBLE IN PARADISE? LOUD CRYING HEARD COMING FROM HOME OF POUND AND PUMPKIN CAKE...

TRICKS UP HER SLEEVE! WE REVEAL THE GREAT AND POWERFUL SECRETS OF TRIXIE!

Soon, Gabby Gums isn't just the talk of Ponyville School, she's a hit all over Ponyville!

Piles of the *Foal Free Press* disappear as ponies line up to get the latest Gabby Gums gossip!

At the beauty salon, the ponies can't stop talking about Gabby Gums.

As Rarity reads aloud from the article CELESTIA: JUST LIKE US?, Twilight Sparkle asks, "Don't you think it's teaching young ponies the wrong lesson? They're embarrassing ponies!"

"Gabby Gums is a hoot!" laughs Applejack.

"I just think Gabby Gums should have more respect for other ponies' privacy! It's not nice to share embarrassing moments or secrets with the entire town!"

The other ponies roll their eyes at Twilight Sparkle.

At the same time, the Cutie Mark Crusaders are starting to feel bad about hurting ponies' feelings. They want to write about their interests again.

But Diamond Tiara will not let them. "We're even bigger than the *Ponyville Express* now!" she exclaims. "Gabby Gums needs to keep delivering the hottest stories in town!"

"Well," sighs Sweetie Belle, "if we want to earn our cutie marks, I guess we have to give the ponies what they want."

Later that week, ponies around town eagerly open the latest issue of the *Foal Free Press*. But their excitement turns to anger as they read the headlines:

PINKIE PIE IS AN OUT-OF-CONTROL PARTY ANIMAL!

APPLEJACK: ASLEEP ON THE JOB!

FLUTTERSHY HAS TAIL EXTENSIONS!

TWILIGHT SPARKLE: I WAS A CANTERLOT SNOB!

"This gossip has become just plain hurtful," says Twilight Sparkle.

Even Rarity has to agree with Twilight when she reads the next headline:

DRAMA QUEEN DIARIES: RARITY'S SECRETS REVEALED!

Suddenly, Rarity realizes that Sweetie Belle is Gabby Gums! Her sister has stolen her diary and published her secrets!

"Sweetie Belle, how could you do this to me?!" Rarity storms into her sister's room. "You're hurting people and invading their privacy! Gabby Gums's nasty news is making ponies feel horrible!"

Indeed, all over town, ponies start to ignore Sweetie Belle, Apple Bloom, and Scootaloo as word gets out that they are behind the Gabby Gums gossip column.

Sweetie Belle, Apple Bloom, and Scootaloo realize if being mean is what it takes to be popular, or to earn a cutie mark, it isn't worth it.

They want to apologize and get their friends back...and Sweetie Belle has a great idea how to do it.

The Cutie Mark Crusaders decide to tell the truth. Gabby Gums publishes her last column:

To tHe CitiZeNs of PonyVille:

I want to apologize for the embarrassment I've caused. My column was actually written by Sweetie Belle, Apple Bloom, and Scootaloo. We got so swept up in earning our cutie marks that we forgot to be nice. But, ponies, we're changing our tune—we promise from now on to respect the privacy of others and not engage in harmful gossip. We hope you'll forgive us, Ponyville.

Signing off for the last time,
Gabby Gums

Sweetie Belle, Apple Bloom, and Scootaloo hand-deliver a copy of the paper with their letter to all the ponies they hurt. It feels good to get hugs from friends and family who accept their apologies.

School has just started for the year, but these ponies have already learned a lot!